JUPITER

KING OF THE GODS, GOD OF SKY AND STORMS

by Teri Temple and Emily Temple
Illustrated by Eric Young

Published by The Child's World®
1980 Lookout Drive • Mankato, MN 56003-1705
800-599-READ • www.childsworld.com

ACKNOWLEDGMENTS
The Child's World®: Mary Berendes, Publishing Director
Red Line Editorial: Editorial direction
The Design Lab: Design and production
Design elements ©: Banana Republic Images/Shutterstock Images; Shutterstock Images; Anton Balazh/Shutterstock Images
Photographs ©: Viacheslav Lopatin/Shutterstock Images, 5; Taras Vyshnya/Shutterstock Images, 8; Shutterstock Images, 13; Daderot, 17; mountainpix/Shutterstock Images, 18; Sergeyussr/Thinkstock, 20; Marcel Clemens/Shutterstock Images, 28; Banana Republic Images/Shutterstock Images, 30

ISBN 9781631437182
LCCN 2014945433

Printed in the United States of America
Mankato, MN
November, 2014
PA02241

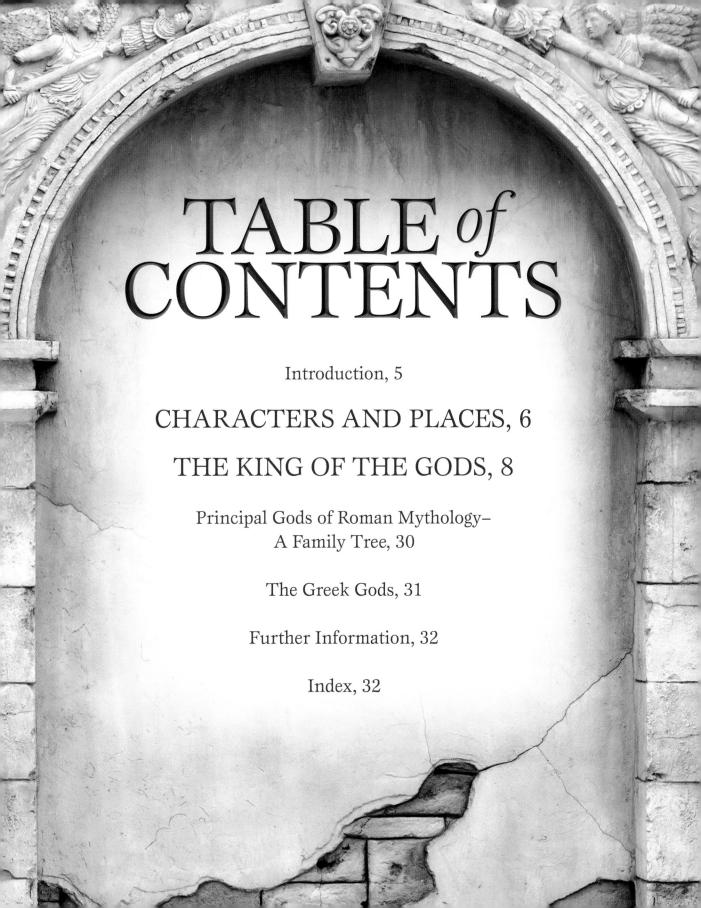

TABLE *of* CONTENTS

INTRODUCTION

In ancient times Romans believed in spirits or gods called numina. In Latin, *numina* means divine will or power. The Romans took part in religious rituals to please the gods. They felt the gods had powers that could make their lives better.

As the Roman government grew more powerful, its armies conquered many neighboring lands. Romans often adopted beliefs from these new cultures. They greatly admired the Greek arts and sciences. Gradually, the Romans combined the Greek myths and religion with their own. These stories shaped and influenced each part of a Roman citizen's daily life. Ancient Roman poets, such as Ovid and Virgil, wrote down these tales of wonder. Their writings became a part of Rome's great history. To the Romans, however, these stories were not just for entertainment. Roman mythology was their key to understanding the world.

ANCIENT ROMAN SOCIETIES
Ancient Roman society was divided into several groups. The patricians were the most powerful and wealthiest group. They often owned land and held power in the government. The plebeians worked for the patricians. Slaves were prisoners of war or children without parents. Some slaves were freed and enjoyed most of the rights of citizens.

CHARACTERS AND PLACES

ANCIENT ROME

ADRIATIC SEA

N
W
S

ROME

TYRRHENIAN SEA

CHAOS (KAY-ahs): *The formless darkness that existed at the beginning of time*

OLYMPIAN GODS (uh-LIM-pee-uhn): *Ceres with daughter Proserpine, Mercury, Vulcan, Venus with son Cupid, Mars, Juno, Jupiter, Neptune, Minerva, Apollo, Diana, Bacchus, Vesta, and Pluto*

TITANS: *The 12 children of Terra and Caelus; godlike giants who are said to represent the forces of nature*

TARTARUS (TAHR-tuh-rus): *The lowest region of the world; part of the underworld; a prison for the defeated Titans and gods*

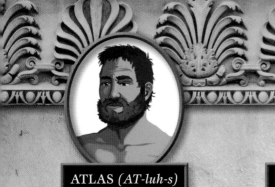

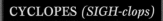

ATLAS *(AT-luh-s)*

A Titan; brother of Prometheus; condemned to support the sky on his shoulders

CAELUS *(CEE-lus)*

The sky and heavens; born of Terra along with the mountains and seas; husband of Terra; father of the Titans, Cyclopes, and Hecatoncheires

CYCLOPES *(SIGH-clops)*

One-eyed giants; children of Terra and Caelus

DEUCALION *(doo-KEY-lee-uh-n)*

Son of Prometheus; survived the great flood and went on to help create a new race of man

HECATONCHEIRES *(hek-a-TON-kear-eez)*

Monstrous creatures with 100 arms and 50 heads; children of Terra and Caelus

JUNO *(JOO-noh)*

Queen of the gods; married to Jupiter

JUPITER *(JOO-pi-ter)*

Supreme ruler of the heavens and of the gods who lived on Mount Olympus; son of Saturn and Ops; married to Juno; father of many gods and heroes

MINERVA *(mi-NUR-vuh)*

Goddess of wisdom and the arts; daughter of Jupiter

OPS *(ops)*

A Titaness; married to her brother Saturn; mother to the first six Olympic gods: Jupiter, Neptune, Pluto, Juno, Vesta, and Ceres

PROMETHEUS *(pruh-MEE-THEE-uh-s)*

A Titan; father of Atlas; gave humans the gift of fire and as a result was punished by Jupiter

SATURN *(SAT-ern)*

A Titan who ruled the world; married to Ops and their children became the first six Olympic gods

TERRA *(TER-uh)*

Mother Earth and one of the first elements born to Chaos; mother of the Titans, Cyclopes, and Hecatoncheires

THE KING OF
THE GODS

Jupiter was the most powerful god in ancient Greek and Roman myths. He became the king of all gods. His story starts with the creation of the universe. In the beginning of time, there was a great nothingness called Chaos. Mother Earth sprang forth from Chaos. She came to be known as Terra. She created the universe.

Terra gave birth to the heavens and the sky, which the Romans named Caelus. Terra and Caelus ruled the world together. They became parents to 12 mighty beings known as the Titans. Later, Terra and Caelus gave birth to three Cyclopes and three Hecatoncheires. Caelus

THE PANTHEON
Ancient Romans had a god for everything in their world. If a farmer hoped for rain, he asked Jupiter to help water the crops. Roman soldiers prayed to Mars, the god of war, for a victory. As a result, there were hundreds of different gods to pray to. Ancient Romans referred to this entire group of gods and goddesses as the Pantheon. They even built a special temple in Rome dedicated to these gods. They also called it the Pantheon.

was fearful of the Titans' great power. He thought his other children were hideous. Each Cyclops had just one eye in the middle of his forehead. The Hecatoncheires had 50 heads and 100 arms. Caelus locked them all deep within the earth so he didn't have to see them. This made Terra angry. She convinced Saturn, one of the Titans, to help her defeat Caelus. Saturn used a special sickle Terra gave him to dethrone his father. Then he set all of his siblings free.

Saturn took the throne as king of the Titans. He married his sister Ops. Their children would eventually become the first six Olympic gods: Vesta, Neptune, Pluto, Ceres, Juno, and Jupiter.

A prophecy foretold that Saturn would suffer the same fate as his father. So when each of his children was born, Saturn swallowed it whole. With his children in his stomach, Saturn thought there would be no trouble.

Ops wanted to free her children, so she devised a plan. When she became pregnant with their sixth child, Jupiter, she snuck away to the island of Crete. Ops gave birth to Jupiter there. She left Jupiter to grow up with the woodland nymphs. When Ops returned to Saturn, she gave him a stone wrapped in swaddling clothes. Saturn swallowed the stone. He thought it was their baby.

When Jupiter was an adult, Ops returned to tell him of his father's evil deeds. Jupiter knew he had to set his siblings free. He went to Mount Olympus, where all of the mighty gods lived. Together with Terra, Jupiter made Saturn throw up all of his children. Jupiter's sisters and brothers were overjoyed. They wanted to help strip Saturn of his power.

Jupiter and his siblings banded together to wage war against Saturn. Saturn had the help of his siblings. Jupiter knew it would be a tough battle for the Olympic gods and him to win. The Olympic gods were powerful. But they needed more help. So Jupiter went to his uncles, the Cyclopes and Hecatoncheires. Both groups agreed to help Jupiter in his quest. The Cyclopes were master blacksmiths. They made weapons for the gods and goddesses to use. The Hecatoncheires were fearsome fighters. The Olympic gods now had powerful allies.

ATLAS

After the battle, Jupiter punished the Titans and their allies. He sent the Titans who fought in the war deep into Tartarus, the underworld. The leader of Saturn's forces was the son of a Titan. His name was Atlas. Jupiter thought he deserved a harsher punishment than the others. For the role he played in the war, Atlas was forced to carry the world on his shoulders for all time.

The fighting lasted 10 years. The battle was so fierce it almost destroyed the entire universe. But Jupiter and the Olympic gods prevailed. As punishment for his wrongdoing, Saturn was sent away from Mount Olympus. Jupiter took his rightful place as king of the gods.

Having finally been freed from their father, the gods and goddesses returned to Mount Olympus. Jupiter lived with his wife, Juno; Neptune; Venus, the goddess of love; and her son Cupid. Jupiter's children, Minerva, Vulcan, Mars, Mercury, and the twins, Apollo and Diana, also lived on Mount Olympus. Jupiter's sisters, Ceres, goddess of the harvest, and Vesta, goddess of the hearth, also helped rule over the world. Together they were the Olympic gods. They lived in a magnificent palace high atop Mount Olympus. Their palace was hidden behind a wall of clouds. Vulcan, the god of fire, and the Cyclopes had built it.

One of the first orders of business was dividing power among the gods. Neptune became the ruler over all the seas. His brother Pluto would hold power over the underworld. And Jupiter would reign over the heavens and earth. With the world finally at peace, the Romans believed the gods protected them.

Jupiter was a strong and respected leader. Ancient
Romans believed he was the god of rain, sky, and thunder.
Jupiter was most often seen with an eagle. The eagle
was his sacred animal. Jupiter was also known to carry

thunderbolts and wear a breastplate, the Aegis, that could ward off any enemy.

Jupiter watched over the heavens and the sky. A mighty chariot called the quadriga carried him around. It was pulled through the sky by four giant horses. Jupiter's thunderbolts helped him keep order. Some ancient Romans believed Jupiter created lightning when he threw his thunderbolts across the sky. They also believed that the sound of thunder came from the rumbling of his chariot and four strong horses. Jupiter was in charge, but his adventures often created trouble. Jupiter was a shape-shifter. This meant he could take on the form of any human or animal. He often transformed himself into the shape of an animal before going down to Earth and interacting with humans.

THE AQUILA
The Aquila is one of the most famous images of ancient Rome. It combines two of Jupiter's symbols. The Aquila is an image of an eagle holding a thunderbolt in its claws. It was the standard, or key symbol, of the Roman army. Standards such as the Aquila were important. They helped soldiers recognize their units in battle. Because of its use in times of war, the Aquila became a symbol of power and honor.

Jupiter loved many women, but he chose his sister Juno for his wife. Juno became the queen of the gods. Juno and Jupiter's first child was Mars, the god of war. He frustrated his parents and caused them much trouble. Their second child was the goddess of youth, Juventas. She would become the cupbearer to the gods and goddesses, which was a great honor. She served food and drinks to all of the gods and goddesses. Vulcan was Jupiter and Juno's third child. He was ugly and deformed, but the gods learned to love him because he was a skilled blacksmith.

VULCAN
Vulcan was the god of fire and blacksmiths. He made weapons, tools, and gifts for the gods. One of these gifts included a bow and arrow for Cupid, the god of love. But Vulcan's gift for Jupiter was the greatest of all. Jupiter asked Vulcan to make him a breastplate that could never be broken. It was the strongest breastplate Jupiter could have wished for. Jupiter called it the Aegis. Vulcan also made Jupiter's thunderbolts.

All three children were very powerful, but none was Jupiter's favorite. Jupiter liked Minerva best. She was also Jupiter's child. Juno did not like her because Minerva had

sprung fully formed from Jupiter's head. Minerva was the goddess of wisdom, war, and arts. Jupiter even entrusted Minerva with his Aegis.

Although he was married and had children with Juno, Jupiter spent time with other goddesses and maidens. This made Juno very angry and jealous. She often took out her revenge on the unsuspecting women.

Jupiter often met and fell in love with beautiful maidens and goddesses. He often had children with these women. One goddess Jupiter visited was the daughter of the Titan Atlas. Her name was Maia. She was a beautiful goddess. Maia easily caught Jupiter's eye. Jupiter snuck away when Juno was sleeping just to see Maia. Maia gave birth to Mercury. He grew up to become the messenger of the gods. Jupiter's sister Ceres attracted his attention next. Their daughter, Proserpine, went on to rule the underworld with her uncle Pluto.

Even though Jupiter tried to be sneaky, not all of the maidens escaped Juno's wrath. A river nymph named Callisto was one of them. Juno turned Callisto into a bear after finding out she had been one of Jupiter's loves. One day Jupiter's daughter Diana killed Callisto. She mistook

URSA MAJOR
Ancient Romans called what we know as the Big Dipper Ursa Major. This means "great bear." People who live in the northern half of the world can see Ursa Major all year long. Today people know Callisto's group of stars as the Big Dipper. This is because several stars within the constellation resemble a large spoon.

Callisto for a real bear. Jupiter placed Callisto in the sky as a constellation of stars.

The Titan goddess Latona was another who barely made it out of Juno's grasp. When Juno found out Latona was pregnant with Jupiter's twins, Juno sent a giant snake after Latona. Latona fled to the island of Delos. There she gave birth to Apollo and Diana. The twins became the god of the sun and the goddess of the moon.

Jupiter fell in love with human females, too. Semele, a princess, was maybe the most unfortunate human. Jupiter fell madly in love with Semele. He swore he would do anything she asked. Juno knew of Jupiter's promise to Semele. So Juno disguised herself as an old nurse. She convinced Semele to ask Jupiter to see him in his splendor, as a god on Mount Olympus. Jupiter pleaded with Semele to change her mind. He knew that any human who saw a god in his or her true form would perish. Semele refused. Jupiter had to grant her wish. He revealed to her his true form. Semele was overwhelmed by it and died.

Juno's jealousy wasn't the only problem Jupiter had to attend to. Other gods often created mischief while he tried to rule the world. One of these troublemakers was the Titan Prometheus.

Prometheus felt bad for the people on Earth. He thought their world was dark and cold. So he stole fire from Mount Olympus and took it to the people of Earth. In return, they used the fire to burn animal sacrifices to thank the gods for their gifts. Jupiter smelled the burning meat. He was angry with Prometheus for stealing fire from the gods. But he loved the smell of the burned sacrifices, so he decided to forgive mankind.

Prometheus, however, was punished for his actions. Jupiter chained Prometheus to a high cliff, where eagles attacked him. Jupiter used unbreakable chains so Prometheus could not escape. Then to spite Prometheus, Jupiter made a human woman named Pandora. He knew Prometheus's brother, Epimetheus, was lonely. Jupiter presented Pandora to Epimetheus as a bride. Pandora and Epimetheus got married. As a wedding gift, Jupiter gave them a box. Epimetheus was worried something bad would be inside. He urged Pandora not to open it. But one day her curiosity got the best of her. She opened the box for a quick peek. When she did, all the fear and evil in the world rushed out. It spread to mankind.

After Pandora opened the box, Jupiter saw that the world was filled with evil. He thought the only way to rid the world of evil was to kill all humans. He decided to do this with a great flood. Prometheus heard of Jupiter's plan. He wanted to stop Jupiter. Before being chained to the cliff, Prometheus had a son named Deucalion. Once a year, Deucalion came to the cliff to visit his father.

Prometheus told his son and his son's wife, Pyrrha, of Jupiter's plan. He told them to build a great chest and fill it with supplies to survive the flood. Pyrrha and Deucalion went to work. As the god of the universe, Jupiter knew what they were doing. But Pyrrha and Deucalion were both faithful to Jupiter. As a result, Jupiter saved them before destroying the rest of the world.

Pyrrha and Deucalion prayed to the gods and asked them what to do. Themis, the goddess of justice, told them it was their job to repopulate the earth. She said they must throw the bones of Mother Earth over their shoulders to make more people. The bones were the rocks of Mother Earth. Pyrrha and Deucalion began throwing stones over

their shoulders. Each stone that hit the ground became a person. In this way, Deucalion and Pyrrha made a new race of men and women on earth.

Jupiter was the leader of all the gods in the Pantheon. The people of Rome believed Jupiter made laws for the land and used them to control Rome. The Romans erected a temple for Jupiter in the center of the Capitol. They used the temple as a meeting place for government business. Astronomers even named a planet after Jupiter. In fact, all of the planets except Earth were named after Roman gods and goddesses. Jupiter, Saturn, Mars, Venus, and Mercury were given their names thousands of years ago. Those were the planets the ancient Romans could see in the sky without a telescope.

Ancient Romans worshipped Jupiter as part of their religion. Over time, a new religion took hold. It was called Christianity.

PLANET JUPITER

Jupiter is the largest planet in the solar system. Jupiter appears as a bright, colorful planet. This is because there are many storms and clouds in Jupiter's atmosphere. It has rings like Saturn, but they are very faint. Jupiter is considered a gas giant. That means it doesn't have a solid surface. It also has 2.5 times the gravity of earth. The red spot you can see with a telescope is often called "The Eye of Jupiter."

Christians refused to worship Roman gods. Soon, worshipping Roman gods was against the law. It wasn't long before Christianity became the dominant religion in Rome. This meant an end for the Roman gods. Gradually, Jupiter and his stories were set aside for new stories. Today these myths and legends teach us about Jupiter and his adventures as king of the gods.

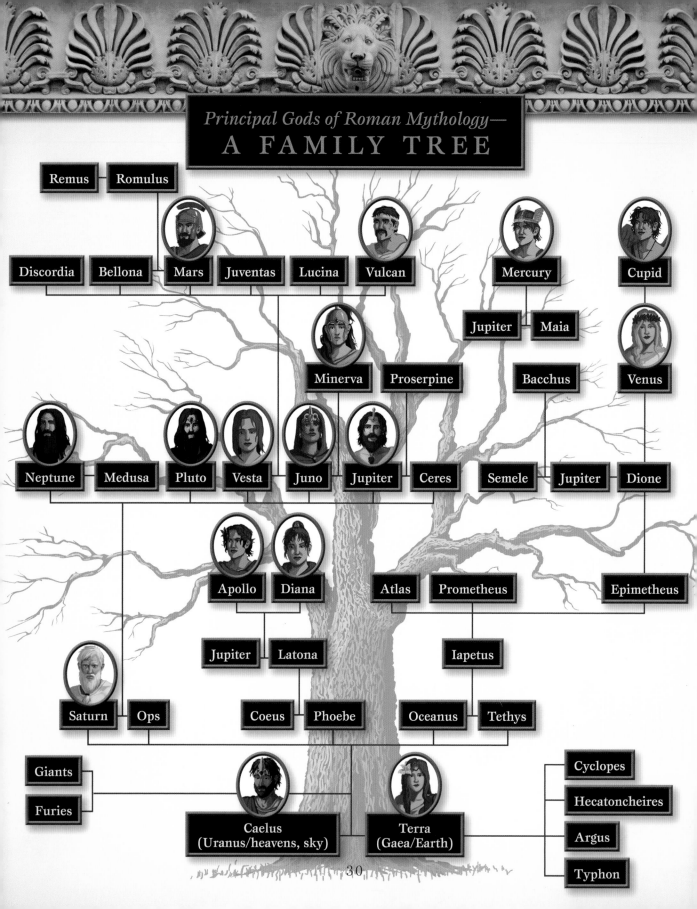

Principal Gods of Roman Mythology—
A FAMILY TREE

Remus — Romulus

Discordia — Bellona — Mars — Juventas — Lucina — Vulcan

Mercury

Cupid

Jupiter — Maia

Minerva — Proserpine

Bacchus

Venus

Neptune — Medusa — Pluto — Vesta — Juno — Jupiter — Ceres — Semele — Jupiter — Dione

Apollo — Diana — Atlas — Prometheus — Epimetheus

Jupiter — Latona — Iapetus

Saturn — Ops — Coeus — Phoebe — Oceanus — Tethys

Giants — Cyclopes

Furies — Hecatoncheires

Caelus — Argus
(Uranus/heavens, sky)

Terra — Typhon
(Gaea/Earth)

THE GREEK GODS

Ancient Greeks believed gods and goddesses ruled the world. The gods fell in love and struggled for power, but they never died. The ancient Greeks believed their gods were immortal. The Greek people worshiped the gods in temples. They felt the gods would protect and guide them. Over time, the Romans and many other cultures adopted the Greek myths as their own. While these other cultures changed the names of the gods, many of the stories remain the same.

SATURN: *Cronus*
God of Time and God of Sowing
Symbol: Sickle or Scythe

JUPITER: *Zeus*
King of the Gods, God of Sky, Rain, and Thunder
Symbols: Thunderbolt, Eagle, and Oak Tree

JUNO: *Hera*
Queen of the Gods, Goddess of Marriage,
*   Pregnancy, and Childbirth*
Symbols: Peacock, Cow, and Diadem
*   (Diamond Crown)*

NEPTUNE: *Poseidon*
God of the Sea
Symbols: Trident, Horse, and Dolphin

PLUTO: *Hades*
God of the Underworld
Symbols: Invisibility Helmet and Pomegranate

MINERVA: *Athena*
Goddess of Wisdom, War, and Arts and Crafts
Symbols: Owl, Shield, Loom, and Olive Tree

MARS: *Ares*
God of War
Symbols: Wild Boar, Vulture, and Dog

DIANA: *Artemis*
Goddess of the Moon and Hunt
Symbols: Deer, Moon, and Silver Bow and Arrows

APOLLO: *Apollo*
God of the Sun, Music, Healing, and Prophecy
Symbols: Laurel Tree, Lyre, Bow, and Raven

VENUS: *Aphrodite*
Goddess of Love and Beauty
Symbols: Dove, Swan, and Rose

CUPID: *Eros*
God of Love
Symbols: Bow and Arrows

MERCURY: *Hermes*
Messenger to the Gods, God of Travelers and Trade
Symbols: Crane, Caduceus, Winged Sandals,
*   and Helmet*

FURTHER INFORMATION

BOOKS

Mincks, Margaret. *What We Get from Roman Mythology.*
Ann Arbor, MI: Cherry Lake Publishing, 2015.

Temple, Teri. *Zeus: King of the Gods, God of Sky and
Storms.* Mankato, MN: Child's World, 2013.

Wolfson, Evelyn. *Mythology of the Romans.* Berkeley Heights, NJ: Enslow, 2014.

WEB SITES

Visit our Web site for links about Jupiter: *childsworld.com/links*

*Note to Parents, Teachers, and Librarians: We routinely verify our Web links to make sure
they are safe and active sites. So encourage your readers to check them out!*

INDEX